DOG DIARIES

ROLF

DOG DIARIES

DOG DIARIES

ROLF

BY KATE KLIMO • ILLUSTRATED BY TIM JESSELL

RANDOM HOUSE 🏠 NEW YORK

The author and editor would like to thank Mary R. Burch, PhD, director, Canine Good Citizen and Therapy Dog Programs, American Kennel Club, for her assistance in the preparation of this book.

All rights reserved. Published in the United States by Random House Children's Books, a division of Penguin Random House LLC, New York.

Random House and the colophon are registered trademarks of Penguin Random House LLC.

Visit us on the Web! randomhousekids.com

Educators and librarians, for a variety of teaching tools, visit us at
RHTeachersLibrarians.com

Library of Congress Cataloging-in-Publication Data
Names: Klimo, Kate, author. | Jessell, Tim, illustrator.
Title: Rolf / by Kate Klimo ; illustrated by Tim Jessell.
Description: First edition. | New York : Random House, [2017] | Series: Dog diaries ; #10 |
Summary: "A dachshund loses his hind leg in an accident and finds his life's calling as a therapy dog" —Provided by publisher.
Identifiers: LCCN 2016010400 | ISBN 978-0-399-55128-4 (paperback) |
ISBN 978-0-399-55129-1 (library binding) | ISBN 978-0-399-55130-7 (ebook)
Subjects: LCSH: Dachshunds—Juvenile fiction. | CYAC: Dachshunds—Fiction. | Dogs—
Fiction. | Working dogs—Fiction. | Amputees—Fiction. | People with disabilities—Fiction. |
BISAC: JUVENILE FICTION / Animals / Dogs. | JUVENILE FICTION / Humorous Stories. |
JUVENILE FICTION / Social Issues / Special Needs.
Classification: LCC PZ10.3.K686 Ro 2017 | DDC [Fic]—dc23

Printed in the United States of America

10 9 8 7 6 5 4

First Edition

For cousin Anna
—K.K.

To the admirable steadiness
and perseverance of dogs
—T.J.

CONTENTS

HOT DIGGITY DOG!

Rolf. That's my name. It's also the sound of my bark. Rich and full-bodied, isn't it? That's because it rumbles up from my powerful chest and booms out of my mouth, like this: *Rolf! Rolf! Rolf!*

Yes, I usually bark in threes. Three is my lucky number. Just why that is, you'll find out if you keep reading my diary.

Go on. Don't be shy. I won't bite. I'm not that kind of dog. What kind of dog *am I*? Long and sleek and handsome. But there's a lot more to me than that.

Rolf is a German name. My breed, dachshund, is also German. But I'm as American as a ballpark frank. That's pretty much the way I'm shaped, too: like a hot dog on four legs. But don't let my amusing shape fool you. It serves a very businesslike purpose. Many hundreds of years ago, German farmers bred us dachshunds to dig and tunnel our way beneath the soil to rout out pests, like badgers. Badger dens are called setts. Sadly, there aren't any badgers (or setts) in my backyard. (Not that I haven't dug up the place many times looking for them.) But let me put it this way: if you're ever in need of Super-Canine Acts of Underground Pest Control, I'm your dog.

I was born in the state of Ohio. The kennel owners were serious about dog breeding, but silly when it came to names. You see, my full name is Rolf von Noodle. Go ahead, laugh. Everyone does. My mother's name was Gertrude von Noodle. Granny was Brunhilda. I have a cousin named Rudy and another named Strudel. You get the idea.

My first companion was a dear, sweet woman. Aunt Agatha was the name she came to. She was everyone's aunt and nobody's mother, except to a long line of von Noodles. I'm proud to say that I was her fifth von Noodle—and she will always be *Mama* to me.

By the time I came to live with Mama in her little house on Cherry Tree Lane, she was nearing the end of her seventh decade. That's a lot of people years, and even more in dog years. Every morning when she woke up, she would groan and say to me, "Rolf, don't ever live to be eighty. Eighty is not for sissies."

At the time, I was just a pup and had no idea what she was talking about. It is only now, as I approach the age of thirteen (a hefty sum in dog years), that I begin to understand what she meant.

When I say that Mama knew dachshunds, I mean she really *knew* us. She knew our strengths and our weaknesses. For instance, dachshunds make a lot of noise, especially considering our size. *Some* people find this not only a weakness, but an irritant. I happen to think it's a strength. But my *rolfing* never bothered Mama in the least. It might have helped that she was slightly deaf. Even so, she understood that I wasn't just making noise. I was protecting her. If I was protecting her from nothing more dangerous than a passing chipmunk or a falling leaf, it didn't matter. What mattered was that I was on the job, always looking out for my Mama.

We dachsies have a tendency to put on weight. And because of our long spinal columns, extra weight is the last thing we need. Mama fed me special food. A man in a truck delivered a bag of it regularly. I considered this gentleman a good friend. Mama liked him, too. She called him the Kibble Fairy.

Mama and I were often sitting out on the porch when the Kibble Fairy pulled up in his truck, with a cheery little *toot-toot-toot*. I always answered with a *Rolf! Rolf! Rolf!* of my own. Being nobody's fool, I gave a warm, friendly *Rolf!*, not the ferocious kind. The Kibble Fairy carried the bag into the kitchen and put it in the lower cupboard, where Mama could get at it easily.

Hot diggity dog, but I loved those bags! They smelled *sweet*! I got one scoopful twice a day. I could have easily eaten three times that amount without missing a beat. But no matter how sad-eyed I looked at Mama, she held fast to the Two-Scoop Rule.

Mama was also a master of the Dachshund Hold. If you've ever held a dachsie, you know that we need special handling. Some people hold us upright like a bag of groceries. Others tuck us under their arm like a football, or sling us over their shoulder like they're burping a baby.

Wrong! Wrong! Wrong! The proper way to hold a dachshund is one hand under the chest, the other around the hindquarters, supporting the back at all times.

Mama kept us to a strict exercise routine. Nothing too strenuous. Lots of brisk walking through the neighborhood. We also played catch with a fuzzy tennis ball in her fenced backyard. Mama needed the exercise as much as I did. If she didn't keep moving, she claimed, she'd seize up like a rusty old combine.

We took three walks a day, giving me a chance to stretch my legs and commune with nature. Mama carried a roll of blue poop bags. Without fail, she'd pick up all my poops and slip them into one of the bags for disposal. In addition to being a sweetie pie, you might say that she was the ultimate responsible dog owner.

Once a week, we visited Madge's House. Madge lived five doors down. There, Mama and Madge and two other friends, Birdie and Betty, played mah-jongg.

Never heard of mah-jongg? It is a strange People Game that involves slippery tiles, fancy little sandwiches, and dainty cups of tea.

With their yippy-yappy little dogs on their laps, Madge, Birdie, and Betty, along with Mama, would laugh and chat and sip and nibble and click mah-jongg tiles.

To her credit, Mama never treated me like a lapdog. My assigned spot during these get-togethers was beneath the table. From down there I had a clear view of the other dogs. And a sorrier slew of specimens you never laid eyes on.

One looked like a small sack of gnawed chicken bones. Another like a child's stuffed toy. The third like a woman's wig in search of a head. They had little in common apart from their yappiness.

And yap they did: at each other, at the old gals, at me, at life! Who could blame them? I'm sure life was no picnic. I mean, where was the adventure? Where was the challenge? More to the point, *where was the self-respect?*

The ladies would reach beneath the table and sneak their little darlings bits of sandwich.

Snap! Snap! Snap! went the yappy little jaws as they accepted their bribes.

Rolf! Rolf! Rolf! went I, each time I caught them in the act. *You, there! Bad behavior, eating people food. You'll be sorry!*

Sez you! arfed the Bag of Bones.

You're just jealous because you never get any, growled the Stuffed Toy.

Go chase your tail, Wiener! snarled the Wig.

Which, naturally, only caused me to step up the *rolfing.*

"Land sakes! Put a sock in it, Rolfie," said Birdie.

"Does he need to use the Little Men's Room?" said Betty.

"For such a small dog, he's *awfully* loud," said Madge.

Did someone say LOUD? I'll show you LOUD.

ROLF! ROLF! ROLF!

Mama would sigh and click her tiles. "I'll bet if you ladies stop sneaking your dogs tidbits, he'll quiet right down. And don't even *think* of giving any to Rolf. I watch what goes into his mouth. As far as I'm concerned, Rolf's body is a temple. A canine temple."

Another of our regular outings would be to visit Mama's nephew, Young Ricky, in his house across town.

Young Ricky's place smelled great: like hamburger and potato chips and sweaty socks. Except for one thing: it also smelled of *cat*. For Young Ricky was one of them.

A Cat Person.

In this world, there are Dog Lovers and Cat People. Notice that I say *People,* instead of *Lovers,* for who, I ask, could ever truly love a cat? Cats are lurkers and loners and critters of the night. Unlike dogs, who are noble and selfless, cats do nothing without having a deeply selfish reason.

Smokey was the name of this particular cat. And true to her name, she would vanish into thin air as soon as we came through the door. Sometime during our visit she would always reappear— *poof!*—just like that, on a high shelf or underneath the couch, and glare at me.

It was eerie, I tell you.

She did everything in her power to make me feel like the world's Least Welcome Guest. I don't know how many times I invited her to come out and play, with an eager *Rolf! Rolf! Rolf!* But the most I ever got out of her was a switch of her tail and a low hiss that said, *If I wanted to, Dog, I could cause you a world of pain.*

Kibble, fetch, walks, mah-jongg, and visits with

Young Ricky and the Feline Mistress of Pain. Such was our life together, Mama and me. A little dull for a lively young pup, you're thinking? What can I say? I'm a sucker for routine. Plus, the world was a vast and uncertain place. And yet I knew one thing for sure: Mama loved me and I loved her back.

I could have gone on this way forever, living with Mama in the little house on Cherry Tree Lane. But fate had other plans.

THE SNEEZE THAT SHOOK MY WORLD

It started out a perfect day. It was early spring, and the scents that had been in a deep freeze all winter long were thawing and calling out to me, *Psst. Rolf! Over here!*

I guess Mama was as eager to get out and about as I was. First thing in the morning, she put on her big white sneakers and her smart sweat suit with stripes down the sides of the legs.

Whipping out my leash, she said, "Come on,

Rolfie, old pal of mine. Let's go to the Dog Park."

Dog Park? Yes! I danced around, my ears flipping inside out with the sheer joy of it.

On the way, I strained at the leash. I sniffed here, sniffed there, taking everything in: the squirrels, the birds, the chipmunks, the grubs, the dirt, the old half of a pastrami sandwich someone had thrown beneath a bush. Everything was music to my nose.

When we finally arrived, I was frisky and ready to roll. I led Mama to my favorite part of the park, the Off-Leash Area. It was a fenced place where we dogs were allowed to run free and hobnob to our hearts' content. You might say it was a lively social scene.

When I first arrived, I stood just inside the gate, ears forward, tail sticking straight out, alert to any threats to me or to Mama. Satisfying myself that all was well, I relaxed and wagged my tail.

Hot diggity dog! I'm back! I announced to the gang.

Buffy, the big, fluffy sheepdog, came frisking over to me.

Hey, Rolf! Good to see you.

Back at you, girl! I said as we gave each other the routine sniff.

Biff, the mastiff mix who was afraid of his own shadow, approached me meekly. Everything on him drooped: ears, tail, eyes. From the fearful way he carried on, you'd think he was the small dog and I was the big bruiser.

Hey, Biff, good to see you, I said.

Is it really? Or are you just saying that?

See what I mean? Biff had serious self-esteem issues.

The corgi triplets had gotten themselves so

knotted up in each other's leads that their walker was down on his knees, working out the tangles. Meanwhile, they leapt around and tried to herd each other. They were some silly sisters, all right.

Bagel and Schmear, the beagle brothers, were kicking up a small cloud as they roughhoused in a dust wallow.

And there was my girl! Gloria, the bashful greyhound, stood off in the corner, shivering and pretending to be invisible.

I romped over to her. She stood as still as a statue while I sniffed her. *Hey, it's me. Your old pal, Rolf,* I said.

Finally, she relaxed. *Where have you been? I've missed you!* she said.

It's been too cold and wet for Mama to come out, I said. *I've missed you, too!*

My tongue was hanging, and my tail was

whipping back and forth so hard my whole back
moved with it. This is what they mean by the tail
wagging the dog.

Wanna race? I said.

You wouldn't think a short-limbed animal like

myself would take on a leggy pro like Gloria. The fact is, I had a highly competitive spirit.

I loved to run, my legs a churning blur. I loved to feel the wind blowing in my ears. And I loved to win, which happened more often than you'd think. You see, my greyhound friend was retired from the track. Her serious running days were behind her. So I just let it rip. *Hot diggity dog!*

We raced back and forth, first me in the lead, then her, then me again, until we tumbled to the ground in a furry heap, me with a big fat smile on my face.

Thanks, I said to her, panting. *I needed that.*

That was when I heard Mama call my name. I leapt to attention.

Gotta go, I said to Gloria. *See you around.*

"You showed that skinny little greyhound what

for," Mama said as she latched my leash back onto my collar. "Time to head back home, young man. We've got company coming tomorrow and a house to clean."

Grrrr. If there's anything I hated, it was cleaning house. I hated everything about it. I hated the vacuum cleaner. I hated the cleaning products in their spray bottles, hissing and filling the air with bad smells. I hated how Mama worked so hard she almost forgot about me.

Why did humans have to clean? If it were up to me, I'd let the dirt pile up. Things smell so much better beneath a few choice layers of grime. At least, that's the way we dogs feel about it.

When the time rolled around for my midafternoon walk, she was still at it, feather duster in hand like a big dead bird. But my bladder was talking to me, and as far as I was concerned, the dust would just have to wait.

Rolf! Rolf! Rolf!

She waved the dead bird at me. "I know, Rolf. We'll go outside in a wee sec. Just let me dust the top of this window frame and I'll be all yours."

She pulled up a small, rickety chair and climbed onto it. What was she thinking? That chair wasn't safe! I made the Worried Dog Sound. You know the one. Halfway between a growl and a mewl. It was the one that was designed to make people stop whatever they were doing and ask, "Aw! What's wrong, little doggie?"

But it wasn't working on Mama. Not today.

The top of the window frame must have been very dirty. Suddenly, the air was thick with dust.

The next instant, the poor woman sneezed so

hard she toppled backward off the chair.

There she lay on the floor, as still as stone.

I ran over and licked her face. She moaned.

Rolf! Rolf! Rolf! I shouted, with no intention of stopping until someone came to help.

It was the Kibble Fairy who finally responded to my alarm. At first, he leaned on the doorbell. That only made me bark louder. He called out, "Miss Agatha? Are you okay?"

That really got me going. I ran over to the living room window and scratched the glass frantically. Finally, he came over and peered in at me. I think he got the message, because after that, he scrambled back to the door and kicked it open.

Things happened very quickly then. A man and a woman soon arrived and put a mask over Mama's face.

Rolf! Rolf! Rolf! I barked, just to let them know who was in charge.

"It's okay, little guy," the woman said to me. "We're trying to help her."

Mama lay on a stretcher, looking very pale. Meanwhile, two of the neighbors wandered over. These ladies never came to visit when Mama was well. What were they doing here now? I switched from barking at the people helping Mama to barking at these two, who were lurking outside the broken-down door.

"I guess we know what all the barking is about!" said the lady from across the street.

"I wonder who's going to take care of him," said the lady from next door. "Do you have someplace to go, little doggie?" She knelt down and poked her nose through the cracked door.

I stopped barking long enough to show my teeth and growl.

Eyes wide with terror, she leapt back. I showed her!

The woman taking care of Mama stepped over me and said through the crack in the door, "Listen, can you ladies look after the dog? Miss Appleton is going to the hospital."

The neighbor women both shook their heads, but one of them said, "She has a nephew who lives across town."

"I think his name is Ricky," said the other. "I can look up his number and give him a call if you like."

LIGHTNING STRIKES

Young Ricky steered his shiny car away from Mama's house. The window next to me was cracked open. Through it, the wind blew in, carrying a Brave New World of Scents. But right now, my nose couldn't handle it. I was already on overload. Where was my Mama? Where was I going? I felt lost and confused.

"Look, Rolf," said Ricky. "I promised Aunt

Aggie that if anything ever happened to her, I'd look after you. I was pretty sure that day would never come. But I don't think she's coming home anytime soon."

I looked at him. His knuckles on the steering wheel were white. His breathing was harsh. His eyes were wide with fear. This was my new companion? I turned back to the window. I missed Mama so badly I wanted to cry.

Ricky chattered on. But I knew that beneath the fake cheer, he was as upset as I was.

"We'll be fine," he said. "You're a small dog—you must be low maintenance, right? If an old lady can take care of you, so can I. And you'll have Smokey to play with during the day. That will be fun for you, won't it?"

No sooner had I set foot in the front door than

the scent of cat nearly knocked me over. What a stink! It hadn't smelled *this* bad when Mama and I had visited.

"Pew!" said Ricky, batting at the air. "This place is rank! I need to change the litter."

I worked my way around the living room, cautiously sniffing. There were traces of cat hair everywhere and footprints that reeked of cat waste. Then I remembered the horrible, disgusting truth. Like many felines, this animal relieved herself inside the house in a box filled with tiny rocks. And cats claim to be clean? Please!

And then there she was, standing in the doorway! Her tail switched, and her eyes burned into me.

If it isn't the Mistress of Pain, I said, swallowing hard.

Where is your person? she asked in a low and cunning voice.

She fell and hurt herself, I told her. *Not that you care.*

Dogs without their people are not to be trusted. You're not welcome.

Believe me, I don't want to be here.

Then why don't you just go?

I would if I could, but this is my home now, too. Can't you just give me a break?

She raised a paw and licked it. Then she sneered, *Typical sucker dog attitude.*

I growled. *What did you say?*

You heard me, Short Pants.

My growl deepened. I was ready to spring. *Did you just call me Short Pants?*

If the pants fit, wear them.

I'll show you, I said, lunging at her.

Oh, you think so, do you?

One moment, I was caught up in a whirlwind of fur and spittle. The next, the cat was gone and I had blood dripping off my nose.

It was more than I could bear. First Mama, then this! I yelped pitifully.

Ricky came running. "Rolf—what did you do to Smokey!"

I want my Mama! I howled, even though I knew Mama couldn't hear me.

After this unfortunate incident, Smokey and I steered clear of each other. She was just a flicker at the edges of my vision. If it weren't for the few chunks of litter that she tracked into my food bowl every morning, I might have thought she'd up and left. But I knew these dirty little bits were a message, and that message was loud clear: *Hit the road, Short Pants.*

Mealtimes posed a different set of challenges— to my digestive system.

"Sorry, Rolf, but I can't afford that fancy dog food Aunt Aggie got you," he told me as he poured kibble into my bowl.

The new food tasted okay, but it gave me the squirts (if you know what I mean). Eventually I got used to it, but it was rough going for a while.

What can I say? I had always thought of myself as tough. But this was a lot for even the toughest dog to handle. There was dodging Smokey, missing Mama, and nursing my rumbling gut.

Let's face it, what with one thing and another, I was one Down-and-Out, Deeply Depressed Dachsie.

Not that Ricky noticed. Such a busy young man! He left the house every morning and didn't come back until the sun was setting—and my bladder was ready to explode. A couple of times, I couldn't hold it in. Much to my embarrassment, I went in the house. Ricky never punished me, though. He just dropped a towel and wiped it up with his foot. It took more than a little mess on the floor to upset Ricky.

Then came the day when he arrived home with his face all wet and shiny. He leaned against the refrigerator and sniffled and moaned and hugged himself. Poor Ricky was a very upset young man. Even Smokey was worried. She rubbed herself against his legs. She looked to me for answers.

What's with the sniveling human?

He's in mourning, I said. *I've seen the signs before. Someone he knows has crossed the Rainbow Bridge.*

I can't tell you how, but I knew that the *someone* was my Mama.

He reached down and stroked Smokey. Then he said to me, "Come here, Rolf, and give me a kiss. She's gone, buddy. We've lost our aunt Aggie."

He sat down on the floor and wept into my neck.

For weeks, I went around in deep mourning. It was all I could do to swallow my food and hold my head up. Life with Young Ricky was for keeps now.

What would become of me?

But I have to say that it wasn't all bad. Every so often, he stayed home. On those days, I got three walks instead of two, and lots of attention. As Smokey hovered in the shadows, Ricky set out to teach me some tricks.

"Any dog of mine has gotta be able to put on a good show," he said.

Ricky was thrilled to discover that I already knew a few basic commands from Mama. I knew Sit, Stay, Heel, Down, and Come. Ricky added to these a few fancier ones: Chase Your Tail (running in a senseless circle), Shake (raising a paw), Hide (lying down with snout buried in paws), Roll Over (pretty much what it sounds like), and Say Please (barking a single crisp *Rolf!*). Ricky always rewarded Say Please with a treat.

Saying Please would prove to be my downfall.

There were times when other young men invaded the house. They came to guzzle fizzy drinks and munch potato chips and hamburgers. They lined up on the couch, jabbing their fingers at a plastic box and leaning toward the television screen as if their lives depended on it.

Gaming, they called it. And it was the only trick they knew how to do, other than Order Pizza.

When not Gaming, they took turns asking me to do tricks, almost always ending in Say Please. My treat would be whatever food was handy: chips, chicken nuggets, and my shameless favorite: cheese from the pizza pie.

The Mistress of Pain would hiss at me from the sidelines. *You'll be sorry. Those short pants of yours are going to burst.*

I hate to say it, but she was right. Mama's Canine Temple was in a state of ruin.

It wasn't long before I started feeling sluggish and bloated. Even Young Ricky noticed. He hauled me off in his shiny car for a visit with Dr. Donna.

She took one look at me and barked at Ricky, "Where is Miss Aggie? What's happened to Rolf? I hardly recognized him, he's gotten so fat."

Ricky cowered. "My aunt passed away recently after a bad fall. Rolf is living with me now."

Dr. Donna's voice softened. "I'm sorry to hear that. She was a lovely lady." Then her voice suddenly sharpened again. "Can I ask what you've been feeding this dog? He's carrying quite a paunch."

"Dog food. And treats. He really likes cheese."

"Okay, listen up: No more treats. No cheese. This dog's got to lose at least three pounds or he'll develop serious back problems."

"Yes, ma'am!"

Like it or not, I was now on a diet. That meant no more treats. Ricky went out and bought me my old special kibble. And he began to take me for long walks in the nearby state park.

"This isn't just for you, Rolf," he said the first time we went there. "I can use the exercise, too."

I'd never been to *this* park before. At first, the wild scents drove me a little crazy. The trees teemed with birds of all kinds. Branches bobbed with squirrels. Chipmunks streaked across the forest floor, *chip-chip-chipping* to pass the warning down the line: *Dangerous Dog at large!*

That was me: a Dangerous Dog. *Rolf! Rolf! Rolf!*

I pulled at my leash. *Let me loose, and I'll show these varmints who's King of this Forest.*

Then one day, while we were walking through the park, I smelled *It*.

I raised my head into the wind to sift through the many scents until I isolated the one I was after. My eyelids drooped. My nostrils quivered. My mouth stretched into a blissful smile. Even Ricky noticed.

He asked me in an excited whisper. "Rolf, what do you smell?"

It was the scent I had been put on this earth to follow. I strained at the end of my leash.

Ricky laughed. "Easy, boy. We're sticking to the

path. There's poison ivy and who-knows-what in those woods."

I continued to tug and pull, my breath rasping. After a bit, Ricky said, "Cool it, Rolf!" And he gave me a good, hard tug of his own.

When he went down on one knee to tighten the lace on his boot, I saw my chance. As soon as I felt the slack in the leash, I yanked myself free.

Hot diggity dog! I was off and running!

"Rolf!" Ricky shouted. "NO! Come, Rolf! COME HERE!"

But I was now listening to another voice. The voice inside my own furry head. That voice said, *Run it to earth!*

Who knows how long or how far I ran on the trail of the scent? Leash whipping behind me, nose to the ground, I followed it deep into the woods until I came to a hole. I poked my head inside and breathed deep.

Rolf! Rolf! Rolf!

This was the scent my dachshund ancestors had been bred to follow. A scent that was in my very blood: *badger!*

I plunged headfirst into the hole. My forelegs transformed into a pair of powerful diggers, tearing away at the earth, widening the hole, bringing me nearer to the badger. My mouth drooled. My head spun. I kicked up a raging dirt storm.

I guess you could say I was having a Moment.

My Moment to perform Super-Canine Acts of Underground Pest Control.

"Rolf! Come, Rolf!"

Ricky's voice was far away now. I barely heard it as I worked my way down into the damp, rich

earth. I was so busy I didn't feel the sky lowering or the temperature dropping or the sun disappearing behind clouds. I didn't hear Ricky's calls growing more and more frantic.

It was only when I stopped to catch my breath

and shake the dirt off my coat that I felt the first cold drop of rain plop onto my nose. It was followed by a whoosh of cold wind that bent the limbs of the trees and carried a thousand new scents.

Distracted, I looked up and sniffed.

Storm!

Overhead, the sky darkened. Then came the rumble of thunder. Some distance away, I saw the sky light up with a dangerous glint.

And—just like that—my Moment had passed, blown clean away by an even more powerful force of nature. Not just any storm, but a *big* rip-roaring electrical storm!

"Rolf! Rolf!" Ricky's voice faintly called. "Come, Rolf! COME!"

I tore myself away from the hole and made my

way back through the woods to the path that led to Ricky.

I saw him up ahead. His face was pale and terrified.

"THERE you are!" He knelt and grabbed the end of my leash. "Let's get out of here NOW."

I led the way back. We were still in the woods when the storm broke over us with full force. Torrents of rain fell. I'd never seen Mother Nature so angry. We raced along the muddy path.

Ricky's was the only car left in the park. Jagged forks of light jabbed at the puddles.

Rolf! Rolf! Rolf! I barked at them. *Get away! How dare you?*

"We gotta make a run for it, bud!" Ricky shouted above the storm's racket.

He scooped me up under his arm and ran to

the car. He swung open the back door and tossed me down on the seat.

An angry fork of lightning speared the ground at his feet. Ricky jumped and screamed.

With a sickening *thunk,* the heavy door slammed shut on my hind leg.

4

MINDY

I have never felt such pain. It was like a wild animal had gotten hold of me and was tearing me apart. I was too stunned to work up a single *Rolf!*

In the front seat, Ricky blew the horn and shouted at other drivers, "Emergency! Clear the way!"

Every time the car dipped into a rut, a fresh wave of agony washed over me.

"Hang on, Rolf!" I heard him say.

He had wrapped me in his jacket. I burrowed down deep into it, trying to hide from the pain. But the pain knew where I was, and it came gunning for me.

Suddenly, Ricky brought the automobile to a jerking halt. I yelped. He opened his door, leaned out, and threw up.

He slammed the door shut and drove on.

"I'm so sorry, Rolf," he said, wiping his mouth on his sleeve.

He must have said those words a thousand times. There was no need. I knew he felt bad. And I had already forgiven him. That's the thing about dogs: we forgive.

I became aware of Ricky talking on his telephone. "His leg got caught in the door," he said.

"It was an accident. There's blood everywhere! It's terrible! I can see the bone and muscles and everything!"

He was silent for a bit, listening. Then he said, "I don't understand. Why can't we come to you? *Rolf knows you.* You know Rolf."

After another silence, he said, "Okay. The animal hospital. Yeah, I'm pretty sure I know where it is. You'll call them and let them know we're coming? Thanks."

He tossed the phone aside and said, "No Dr. Donna for this. You're heading straight for the animal hospital. Hang in there, bud. I'll get you there as fast as I can."

I must have passed out, because I woke up to Ricky lifting me out of the car. I let out a few yelps. I couldn't help myself. Even though he was being gentle, it still hurt like the blazes. He ran through the rain into a long, low building. My nostrils took in a sharp medicinal smell mixed with the sad stink of suffering animals.

A young woman met us at the door. She was standing next to a high table with wheels. "Donna's office called. They're ready for you. Set him down here," she said. "Easy, now. The less we jostle him the better."

"Are you the doctor?" he asked.

"No," she said. "I'm Mindy. I'm a volunteer. Hey, Rolf," she said. She didn't touch me, but her calm, soft voice felt like the first healing touch. "Don't worry, little guy. The doc's gonna take away all the pain and fix you up like new. You'll see."

Suddenly, a big man in a white coat loomed over me. "Let's see what we've got here," he said.

Slowly, he peeled away the bloody jacket.

"Oh, God!" Ricky gasped. "Is he going to make it?"

"What's the dog's name, sir?" the man asked.

Ricky sputtered and shook his head.

"It's Rolf, right?" Mindy said to Ricky.

Ricky blubbered. "Yes. Rolf. He was my aunt's dog. She passed away and left me to take care of him. I promised her I'd take care of him and now look. I'll never forgive myself if he dies."

"Mindy, can you show this young man to the waiting room? I'll get an IV started on Rolf. Try not to be so hard on yourself, sir. Accidents happen, and this dog will need all your strength if he's going to recover."

The man wheeled me into a room with blinding bright lights. I felt a sharp pinch and then nothing.

I woke up lying on the same table. Lights shone down on me. They were as warm and bright as the sun. Tubes ran in and out of me, and a machine nearby beeped. The big pain was gone, replaced by a smaller one I could manage. My head swam and my leg ached, but I couldn't lick it because I was strapped down so tight.

Strapped onto the table next to me was a large, shaggy dog with a white bandage on his front leg.

You awake? he said in a gruff voice. *You were down for the count.*

Huh—what? My head was still reeling. *Am I alive?* I asked.

Looks like it to me, pal. What are you in for?

I'm not sure. I think Ricky shut my leg in the door of his car.

A car door? You don't say? That wasn't very smart

of him, no offense to this Ricky fellow.

Bit by bit, it was beginning to come back to me: the badger, the breakaway, the storm, the car door, the pain.

It was an accident. The lightning made him do it. Why are you here?

I chase cars, he said.

Cars? Do you catch them?

No. But it's not for lack of trying, he said.

Looks like one caught you, I said.

You're right about that, he agreed with a weak chuckle. *This is the second time I've been tagged by a fender. As soon as I chew this cast off, I'm going to catch one if it kills me.*

Keep it up and it just might, I said. Some dogs just don't have the brains God gave geese.

Still woozy, I drifted off to sleep again.

When I woke, my roomie was gone. So were the tubes, along with the beeping machine. Sitting in a chair nearby was Mindy. She was looking at me most intently while she drew on a pad of paper.

"Rolf—you're awake! I hope you don't mind me sketching you. You look so sweet and peaceful. Feeling better?"

I struggled to sit up, but the straps wouldn't let me.

She set aside her pad and stood up. "I'll go get the doctor."

A man in a white jacket peered in my eyes with a bright light. "He's bounced back nicely. I think we can move him out of recovery and into the kennel. But let's get an Elizabethan collar on him first. We don't want him messing with that incision until it's had time to close. And we *know* you'd love

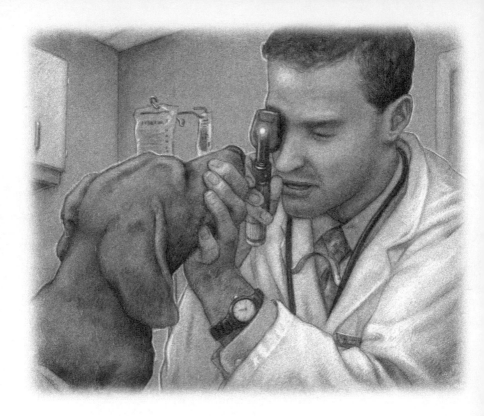

to do that, don't we, Rolf?"

They unstrapped me and fastened a stiff, plastic cone around my neck. I moved my head around, craning to take in my surroundings. But the collar made it difficult. I guess that was the idea.

Then they wheeled me off to a room that was stacked with cages. Almost all the cages were occupied. There were dogs and cats. I even caught a whiff of a rabbit.

They put me in one of the lower cages, on the floor. It was spanking clean, with a soft bed in the corner and a bowl of water. But a cage is still a cage. And if it weren't for my wooziness, I might have given out with a *Rolf!* or two. But all I really wanted to do was sleep.

Making myself as comfortable as I could, I curled up and did just that.

Often when I woke up, Mindy was there with a bright smile and a kind word. But where was Ricky?

"I think Ricky's afraid to come see you, Rolf," Mindy said one day. "I've seen this reaction before.

He must feel so guilty. Plus, he's probably a little squeamish about your leg. But he'll get used to it, you'll see."

Mindy soon began to take me out of the cage. She would sit on the floor a short distance away from me and ask me to come to her.

It was one of the first tricks Mama had taught me—Come—and one of the easiest. But when I tried walking toward Mindy, my legs wouldn't obey. Instead of walking like a normal dog, I hopped, skipped, and jumped. It wasn't pretty, but I made it to her all the same. Mindy always rewarded me with a cuddle and a smile. No one had cuddled me since Mama. I couldn't get enough of those Mindy cuddles.

It was during this time that I stopped barking quite so much. At first, it was because it hurt my

leg to bark. But then I think it was because Mindy
made me feel safe. I even liked the way she smelled.
After a few days, she was all that was important to
me. Nothing else registered on my *rolf*-o-meter.

Can you guess what was happening to us? You
got it. Mindy and I were falling in love.

TRIPOD

I was glad that Mindy was there when Ricky finally came.

"Oh, wow," he said when he first saw me. Then he turned away quickly, as if he couldn't stand the sight of me.

If you want to know the truth, I wasn't all that thrilled to see him, either. Compared to Mama, and now to Mindy, he was not my idea of the perfect partner. Were we going to be picking up where we left off? I sure hoped not.

"Did you talk to the doctor?" Mindy asked.

"Yeah, I did," he said. "He gave it to me straight."

I kept waiting for Ricky to pet me or talk to me. I mean, hadn't we been buddies? Sort of? But he didn't touch me. And he talked only to Mindy. I didn't pay much attention to what they were saying. I was still a little muddled and didn't understand most of it. They used words I didn't know, like *post-surgical incision* and *amputation* and *tripod*. I put my head down on my paws and dozed while they droned on.

"Most tripods don't even mourn the loss," Mindy was saying. "When humans lose a leg, it's a big deal. Dogs still have three left. Plus, humans care what they look like. Dogs don't. You'd be sur-prised how quickly they adjust."

"Yeah," Ricky said, "but can their masters ad-just? That's the question."

"Do you have a *problem* dealing with this?" Mindy asked.

I opened my eyes when Ricky began to pace.

"Look," he said, "maybe it was a mistake for me to keep him. I'm not a dog person. I could barely care for him before. How am I supposed to do it now that he's . . . like this?"

Ricky stopped and turned to Mindy. "You know so much. Maybe you can tell me: are there people out there who, like, *rescue* dogs in his condi-tion? I'd be willing to pay someone to take care of him. Really, I'd pay any amount of money. I'd do anything."

"I've got a great idea, Ricky," Mindy said.

"Why don't you give a big donation to the Dachshund Rescue Society?"

Ricky's eyes glowed. "Really? Do you think they'd take him?"

"Of course they would," she said. "But they don't *have* to. *I'll* take Rolf. It will be my honor and privilege. Rolf is an *amazing* dog. He's strong and intelligent and plucky, and he's got more courage in one *toe*, no offense, than you'll ever have in your entire body."

I still didn't know exactly what was going on here. But I had the sneaky feeling that Ricky was out and Mindy was in.

And that was A-okay with me!

A few days after I had left the hospital and was living with Mindy in my new home, she removed the cone from around my neck.

Ta-da! I could see again!

The first thing I did was turn around to lick my wound. I had been dying to get at it.

That was when I saw—my rear leg was *gone*! Completely vanished!

Say, what was the big idea?

Someone had taken my leg while I was in the hospital! So *that* was what Mindy and Ricky had been talking about. Me! *I* was a tripod!

I know it sounds strange. You'd think I'd have known that my own leg was missing. But the cone had blocked my view. And the strangest thing was, I still *felt* the leg. Many years later, *I still feel it*, like a ghost following the three survivors. And I could get around fine on three legs. I felt better than ever. The fact is, I knew I was lucky to be alive. And lucky to have Mindy. I think she felt pretty lucky,

too. She tied a spiffy blue bandanna around my neck and called me her Mellow Fellow. I had a lot to be mellow about.

Mindy worked at home, for one thing, so she was with me all the time. She sat at a drawing table by a window that looked out on her backyard. She called herself a Children's Book Illustrator. That means she drew pictures of all different kinds of scenes and objects. But it was her dog pictures that were the best. She could draw a dog so lifelike it practically barked at you. It made me want to go up and sniff it.

When she wasn't at her drawing table, Mindy was fussing over me. She put a salve on the scar where my leg had been removed. I don't know why she bothered. I always licked it off. Licking the scar was my main job in those early days out of the hospital. Mindy would scold me when she caught me doing it, but I found ways to sneak in the licks. She also waxed my paw pads. I didn't like it at first, until I realized the wax kept me from slipping on her polished floors.

In no time at all, Mindy and I were walking around the block. It was a breeze. You'd be surprised how much easier it is for a male dog to relieve himself without having to lift a leg. Our walks lengthened until we were soon walking all the way into town.

And one fine day, we even went to the Dog Park. I immediately led Mindy over to the Off-Leash Area, where the old gang was still hanging out.

As soon as they saw me, they came running over: Buffy and Biff and the corgis and the beagle brothers.

They gathered around me and sniffed.

There's something different about you, said Biff, *but I can't quite put my paw on it.*

Sure there is, said Buffy. *He's got a new companion. And she's great!*

They all sniffed at Mindy and agreed she was great.

You're probably wondering why they didn't notice the missing leg. As far as they were concerned, I was still the same old Rolf. That's the way it is with us dogs.

And then I saw her, over in the corner like the old days, shivering and pretending she was invisible. It was my old pal Gloria.

I ran over to her. *Aren't you going to say hello?* I asked, wagging away.

I've missed you, she said bashfully. *Where have you been?*

Around the block a few times, that's for sure. I've learned some tough lessons and suffered some hard knocks, but I'm still here, aren't I?

She touched her nose to mine. *You look pretty good to me. I don't suppose you'd like to race?*

Hot diggity dog! Would I ever!

And—just like that—I was in the running again, racing up and down the Off-Leash Area with Gloria the greyhound at my heels. Whether she let me win because she was a lady, or whether on three legs I was still as fast as ever, I'll never know. All I knew was that it felt good to be back on track.

On the way home from the Dog Park, we stopped at the café. Called Paws to Refresh, it welcomed dogs and their companions. There was a dog underneath nearly every table, and bowls of fresh water were on the house.

Mindy and I sat at a table in the shade of a chestnut tree. A woman and her dog sat at the table next to us. The dog was a good-looking German shepherd. She lay with her eyes closed and her head on her paws.

There was a distinct air of mystery about her.

Before long, Mindy and the shepherd's owner got to talking, as dog owners do. So I decided to make the first move with the Woman of Mystery herself.

Greetings, cousin, I said to her (since we were both German breeds).

She lifted her head and then put it back down as if it were too heavy to hold up.

You seem kind of tired.

She sighed deeply. *I am. But in the best possible way. We visited the children's ward this morning. Those kids really tire me out.*

You play with kids? I asked.

Well, they call it therapy. I'm a therapy dog.

You don't say! I sat up a little straighter. How impressive. This dog was a professional woman! Mindy and I enjoyed watching shows on television about dogs who performed all sorts of jobs: helping blind people, sniffing out bombs, finding lost children. But this therapy business sounded like it was right up my alley.

Yes—I visit people in hospitals and other places to help cheer them up.

Meanwhile, Mindy was deep in conversation with the shepherd's companion. She had moved over to sit at her table.

"I've been watching you with your dog," the other lady said. "I bet he'd make a great therapy dog."

"Do you really think so?" Mindy asked. "I'm curious. Why do you think that? His missing leg?"

"Well, that's one reason. He's a great example of someone overcoming hardship. But really it's you *and* the dog. You've obviously got a great bond with him. And I've noticed he's very good around everyone and everything: other dogs, strangers, kids, traffic, loud noises. Next to my Alice, he's the most mellow dog here."

"He's my Mellow Fellow," Mindy said, giving me a fond pat.

The woman handed Mindy a piece of paper.

"This is the number for the woman who runs the therapy dog class. Her name is Gail. She's also the leader of an outstanding therapy organization in town. Give her a ring, and see if you like what you hear."

"We just might do that," said Mindy. "Right, Rolf?"

I sat up and wagged my tail.

I Become a Good Citizen

I lay at Mindy's feet in a room that was, I tell you no lie, wall to wall with dogs and their companions. The people were seated in rows of creaky metal chairs. Many of the dogs were nosing around, asking each other what was going on. I didn't know any more than they did. I kept my eyes on Mindy. As always, I would take my cue from her.

A woman stood talking at the front of the room. She told us her name was Gail. Lying next to her was a collie named Pal, who had a quiet, composed air about her that reminded me of my German shepherd friend, Alice.

Gail was saying, "Many of the dogs in this room will probably not wind up being therapy dogs."

A murmur ran through the crowd. The dogs looked worried.

"But that's perfectly okay! Your dog may not be suited to this work. Not every dog is. Whatever happens, it's important that you appreciate the vitally important service your dog renders *you* every day of his life. For this reason alone he deserves all your love and respect."

Mindy looked down at me with soft, shining eyes, and I returned the look. Hot diggity, dog diggity, but I loved this girl! I'd do anything for her—and she knew it.

Gail continued. "So what exactly does a therapy

dog do? Consider these scenarios: A child temporarily forgetting the pain of chemo treatment when a dog performs tricks just for her. Hands gnarled with arthritis stroke a dog's soft fur and remember a long-ago beloved pet. A dog sitting before a walk-assist treadmill offers encouragement to a wounded veteran to put one foot in front of the other. A young man who has lost everything he owns in a hurricane finds comfort burying his face in the neck of a dog.

"These are just some of the services a therapy dog can deliver. A good therapy dog can touch many lives: physically, emotionally, and spiritually. But she can't do this in a vacuum. She needs *you,* her human partner, to support her, protect her, and tune in to her at all times. You can't just toss your dog into the fray and expect her to perform miracles. It doesn't work that way."

Heads all over the room were nodding. Faces were serious.

"So what exactly *is* a therapy dog? A therapy dog is a dog who volunteers with his or her human to make a difference in the lives of others. A therapy dog enters hospitals, rest homes, rehab facilities, schools, funeral homes, and disaster sites. Your job is to protect your dog from the stresses that come about as a result of this interaction. You need to observe your dog carefully, making sure he's okay with what's going on. If necessary, you will remove him from any situation that overtires, frightens, or threatens him. Your job requires enormous presence of mind, poise, and judgment. It is a huge responsibility. But it's also, as Pal and I can tell you, a source of unending joy and satisfaction."

Mindy looked down at me and winked. I heaved a sigh. All was well.

"Now, what makes a great therapy dog? That's hard to say. Different dogs bring different gifts to the job. But a strong bond of trust between you is absolutely essential. Today, we're going to test that bond with a little exercise. We're going to ask each of you, one by one, to leave this room. You're going to walk down the hall, and while you're doing that, we're going to give each of your dogs what we call the Bump Test. Let's start with this row here."

The first person and dog in the front row got up and left the room. They came back a few minutes later. The person and dog seemed fine. Then the next person and dog left. And on it went, down the rows. Some of the dogs and people came back into the room looking a little shook up. Others were cool and calm. I wondered what was going on. But when Mindy rose to stand, I got up and went with her. Whatever they were dishing out, I could take.

The hall outside the room was crowded with people—grown-ups and children. Mindy and I joined the crowd. We were walking along when, suddenly, someone bumped me from behind. It didn't hurt, so I thought nothing about it. I just kept on walking and minding my own business.

The thought occurred to me: *Is this the test?* If so, it wasn't very difficult. They didn't even ask me to do tricks! We turned around and went back into the big room.

When all the dogs and people had left and come back, the woman named Gail said, "What you and your dogs just underwent was what we call bumping. It's when one of us comes up behind your dog while he's walking with you and very gently bumps into him. If your dog just kept on going, he's got the makings of a good therapy dog. If your dog barked or whipped around and growled, then maybe you need to think again about being a therapy team.

"Of course, it's not the be-all and end-all of tests. But I've found that it's a pretty good indicator of a dog who has what it takes to do therapy work. What *does* it take? First of all, trust. Your dog must trust his human partner. Second of all, grace. Your dog must display grace under pressure. Third of all, willingness. Your dog must be willing to cooperate with the program, whatever it may be."

Over the next two months, we returned to this room many times. We performed the usual obedience exercises: Sit, Stay, Down. There was a great deal of brushing and cuddling, from Mindy and friendly strangers. On a few occasions, strangers even had the nerve to brush my fur the wrong way. *And* fiddle with my ears. But Mindy's look always told me these people didn't know any better, so I forgave them and let it pass.

Do not ask me why, but many serious attempts were made to make me lose my cool. There were loud clanging noises. Heavy objects dropped on

the floor. People rolling past me in wheelchairs or swinging along on sticks or making funny noises and faces. Did any of this bother me? Of course not! I had survived a Vicious Dog-Eating Car Door! This was nothing.

Then there came the field trips. In small groups, we trooped through all sorts of strange-smelling places, like hospitals for children and wounded soldiers and homes for the elderly. In all of these places, we were expected to behave like furry little ladies and gentlemen. Some dogs couldn't hack it and had to be taken away. Through it all, Mindy kept her eye on me and constantly let me know, in her way, that it would be well worth it in the end. I began to take some pride in my ability to handle any situation that came up.

I heard the phrase Canine Good Citizen more than once during this time. And there came a day when Mindy received a piece of paper that made her throw her arms around me and crow with delight.

"You made it! You're not only a Canine Good Citizen, but you're accepted to Gail's therapy group. I'm so proud of you, Rolf! I'm going to frame this and put it on my wall."

It was official: I had joined my friend Alice. I had joined the working ranks. I was a therapy dog.

CALLING DR. ROLF

Mindy turned off the car engine and scooted back the seat. "Together Time, Rolf." She patted her lap. I scrambled into it. And for a few moments, we sat in the hospital parking lot and quietly adored each other.

We cuddled. I licked her face. She scratched behind my ears.

After a while, she sat back. "What do you say, Rolf? Are we ready to roll?"

Ready and steady! Hot diggity dog!

We entered the huge hospital through sliding doors.

The uniformed man at the desk looked up as we approached.

Mindy said, "Good morning. I'm Mindy, and this is Rolf. We're here to volunteer." She took a piece of paper out of her purse and showed it to him.

The man peered at the paper, then at me. "Right, a therapy dog. Know where you're headed? Need directions?"

"Rehab floor," Mindy told him. "We know the way. We came last week with Gail and she watched us work. I guess we did okay, because we're here on our own today."

"Good luck to you both," said the man. "And have a nice day."

We walked down the hall to the elevator. It *pinged* as the doors slid open. People and equipment were crammed inside.

"That's okay. We'll take the next one," Mindy said.

The elevator left without us.

There are few things a dachshund dislikes more than being squeezed into a small space with a large crowd. Mindy was thoughtful that way. The next elevator was empty. We stepped in and, moments later, got out on a different floor.

"This is it, Rolf." Mindy took a deep breath. So did I. Together, we walked down the hall. A set of doors swung open, then closed behind us.

The now-familiar scents surrounded me: medicine, cleaning products, food, people, sickness. They might make some dogs anxious, but I was used to them.

Mindy spoke to a woman standing behind a high desk. Her name was Kim. She seemed thrilled to see us.

"Irene told me about the new therapy dog. I was off last week and didn't get a chance to meet him."

"Yeah, we're kind of newbies, but so far so good," Mindy said.

Kim peered over the desk at me. I wagged my tail and looked up at her.

"Hey, little guy," said Nurse Kim.

"His name is Rolf," said Mindy.

"Rolf. That's a good name for him."

Nurse Kim came around the desk. She was wearing clean white sneakers that squeaked on the shiny floors.

She knelt and petted me. "I hear you were a big hit last week. Everyone loved your tricks. They'll be so happy to get a repeat performance, Rolf."

"We can do that, can't we, Rolf?" Mindy said.

I wagged my tail, always happy to please.

Kim was saying, "He's such a great role model for people in rehab, especially the ones who've lost the use of a limb. My cousin's dog lost his hind legs to bone cancer. He uses one of those rear-support wheelchairs, and he zips around in it. But you don't need one of those, do you, Rolf?"

"No," said Mindy. "Tripods generally do fine on three legs."

"Would you mind visiting a couple of private rooms before you head down to the lounge?"

"Sure. So long as we keep it short. He'll need to save his energy for the big group."

"Absolutely. It's just that these two people put in special requests. And it would be a shame to disappoint them. I'll introduce you, then stick around in case you need me. How does that sound?"

"Perfect," said Mindy.

We followed her down the corridor to a room where we met Mr. McCarthy.

He was sitting in a wheelchair. I approached and sniffed his toes. He had only one set. The other set was missing, along with his leg to just above the knee.

"So this is the famous three-legged dachshund I've been hearing about," said Mr. McCarthy.

"His name is Rolf. Would you like to pet him?" Mindy asked.

"I sure would. Mind if I hold him in my lap?" he asked.

"Of course not," said Mindy.

Mindy pulled a chair up alongside the wheelchair. She settled me into Mr. McCarthy's lap, still holding my leash.

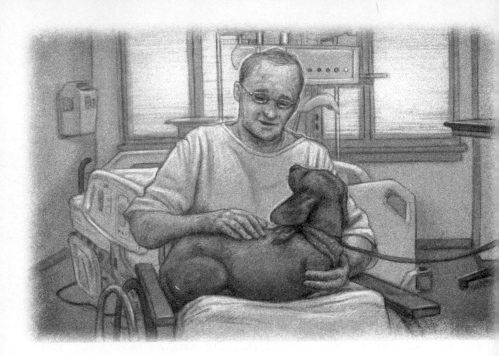

"Hey there, little fellow. I see we're both in the same boat. I got a blood clot and lost circulation. They had to chop off my leg just like they did to you." He ran his hand down my back very slowly. "You've got one silky coat."

"I bathe him once a week," said Mindy.

"I bet he hates that," said the man.

"Not really. I use a mild soap so it won't dry out his skin. It gives us time together. Keeping clean is part of being a therapy dog."

"You don't say. Can we get rid of the leash?" he asked.

"Sorry," said Mindy. "Hospital rules say it has to stay on."

"That's too bad. My dogs never had leashes. We let dogs run free when I was a boy. I grew up thinking leashes were cruel," said the man. "Like a prisoner's shackles."

"The way I see it, it's a bond that holds us together. When he wears his leash, he knows I'm with him. Like a canine umbilical cord."

"I never thought of it that way," Mr. McCarthy said, smiling.

Our next visit was to a woman who was lying

in bed, propped up on pillows. Nurse Kim introduced her as Mrs. Rossi. Her face lit up when we came in the room.

"Would you like to cuddle with the dog?" Mindy asked in a soft voice.

The woman nodded. Mindy set me down on the bed alongside her. Mrs. Rossi lifted her hand and touched her chest. "Put him here," she said faintly.

After putting a sheet over the bed linens to keep them clean, Mindy laid me down on Mrs. Rossi's chest so that my nose was just beneath her chin.

"Ah!" the woman whispered. "I've got myself a doggie angel!"

I stayed with her until she fell asleep with a sweet smile on her face.

Did I fall asleep? Nope. Because I was working.

"Okay, Rolf," Mindy whispered to me as she lifted me off Mrs. Rossi. "It's showtime."

"Hey, folks!" said Nurse Kim as we walked into the lounge. "Here's the Amazing Rolf and his companion, the Marvelous Mindy!"

There was scattered clapping. It was a bright, sunny room with lots of windows. The patients sat in wheelchairs arranged in a half circle. One wheelchair was off to the side, however, away from the group. The man in it was so still and lifeless I thought he might be dead.

I made the worried sound, deep in my throat, and looked to Mindy.

"It's okay, Rolf. Go up and say 'hi' to the man."

I went over and sniffed his feet. There was no movement. Not even a twitch. My eyes traveled up his body. *Aha!* His eyes were open, and he was definitely alive. I noticed his one finger move. It seemed to be waving at me. Or just maybe . . . wanting to shake?

I lifted my paw.

Mindy said to the man, "I think Rolf wants to shake your hand."

The man didn't say anything. One of the other patients said, "Don't expect much from him. He's completely paralyzed. Except for that finger."

"I see," said Mindy.

Another man made his wheelchair spin. "Never mind about that. Come on, Rolf. Let's see some of *your* tricks."

I felt everyone's eyes on me. I looked up at Mindy.

"Are you ready, Rolf?"

I dipped my head, which was my quiet way of saying yes.

She held up her hand as if there were a treat in it, but I knew better. "Rolf. *Sit.*"

And so we began the familiar series of tricks I had first learned from Mama and Young Ricky and perfected with Mindy.

When we were done, she gave me a treat— a crunchy piece of freeze-dried liver. I chewed it up and licked my chops.

The people clapped. Those who couldn't clap smiled. I looked over and saw that the man in the corner was moving his finger again. I had the feeling that he was asking me to Come.

I went over to him.

His finger dipped.

I sat.

His finger dipped further.

I lay down.

His finger lifted.

I stood.

His finger twirled.

I chased my tail.

His eyes closed.

I hit the floor and hid my eyes, peering up at him for the next cue.

His finger rose.

I took to my feet and said, *Rolf!*, which meant *please.*

This time, the clapping was louder and the smiles even wider. Mindy rewarded me with a second liver treat, although I would have done it for free. Because when I looked back at the man, his eyes were shining.

After that day, we were invited to return often to the rehab floor. Each time we did, I ended my visit by performing tricks for the Man with the Finger. It was like he had become as much a part of the show as I was.

One time, a woman in a white jacket came to watch. Afterward, she spoke to Mindy.

"It's remarkable," she said. "I've never seen

anything like it. For the first time, Bill realizes the power he holds in that one finger."

The next time we came to visit, the Man with the Finger's hand was taped to a board on the arm of his chair. His finger tapped a pad. The pad was attached to a screen.

"Bill talks to us now," said Nurse Kim. "He expresses himself by tapping out words with his finger. See on the screen? He's written a message. I think it's for you," she said, looking at me with a smile in her eyes.

Mindy leaned over and read aloud from the screen: " 'Thank you, Dr. Rolf.' "

HAPPY ACRES

I noticed it as soon as I entered the new building.

The smell was familiar: faded flowers, warm milk and chocolate, talcum powder. And then I realized what it was. I was smelling Mama! My dear, sweet Mama.

"We call this a skilled nursing facility, Rolf," Mindy had told me, after our Together Time in the parking lot. "We're going to see how you like it before we make any kind of commitment to paying future visits."

A tall man led us to a lounge filled with sunlight. People sat around at tables and in wheelchairs. After the man announced us, Mindy and I began to make the rounds.

The first person we met was small and wrinkly and looked as if he might slip out of his wheelchair. Then I saw that he was strapped in.

"Do you like dogs?" Mindy asked.

"What's that?" the man grumbled.

"DO YOU LIKE DOGS?" Mindy said, louder.

I glanced at her, wondering why she was raising her voice. Was she mad? Was she scared? She seemed perfectly calm.

"NO, I DON'T LIKE DOGS!" the man yelled back at her. "I'm here to watch TV. If I knew there was going to be a dog show this afternoon, I would have stayed in my room. I have a good mind to complain to the management. What kind of a joint are they running here? This ain't no kennel."

"Okay!" Mindy said sweetly. "Have a nice day, sir."

We stopped at a card table where a frail older woman sat, dealing cards to herself and humming cheerfully.

I lifted my nose to the air. She smelled familiar.

"Do you like dogs?" Mindy asked.

The woman looked up from her game.

"Are you kidding me, honey? I never in my life was without a dog. But when my last little boy met his maker, I didn't have the heart to replace him. Turned out to be a good thing, too, because my daughter didn't think I was safe living alone anymore—*ha!*—and next thing I knew, I was here. At Happy Acres, or whatever this place is called."

Now I knew who this was! This was Mama's friend Birdie, from the mah-jongg days.

Birdie glanced down at me. "My friend Agatha always had dachshunds. I see yours is missing a leg, poor little fella, although he seems pretty healthy and happy to me."

I wagged my tail. *Rolf! Rolf! Rolf!*

Her eyes opened wide, and she set down her cards. "*Rolf?* Is that you? Well, I'll be!"

Mindy laughed. "His name *is* Rolf."

"Oh, he's Rolf, all right. I'd recognize that bark anywhere. Are you Ricky's wife? I'm not being nosy. I know Rolf went to live with him, is why I'm asking."

Mindy shook her head. "No, I'm not his wife.

Ricky decided not to keep Rolf. And I was lucky enough to adopt him."

"So what happened to his leg?" She gestured to my scar.

"He had an accident when he was with Ricky."

She wagged her head and sighed. "I could have guessed. Nice young man. But dumber than a box of rocks, although I would never have said so to Agatha. She doted on him. I remember when she told me she had made Ricky Rolf's guardian. 'Don't do it, Aggie,' I told her. 'He's a cat person. That boy wouldn't know what to do with a dog if it bit him.' But did she listen?"

Birdie leaned down and stroked my fur. "I'm glad to see you landed on your feet, Rolf, even if you only have three left."

She laughed wheezily and began to cough.

"Oh, this little guy was something, all right. He'd sit beneath our game table and lord it over all the other dogs. He was quite the bossy britches, weren't you, Rolfie? Every time one of us would sneak a bite to our doggies, Rolfie, here, would rat us out. And then Aggie would give us a lecture on how Rolf's body was a temple and she would never sully it with tea sandwiches or human food of any description. That was Aggie for you, may she rest in peace. Very serious about the care of her canine companions."

Birdie gave me a kiss on the nose before we moved on to the next person. I didn't like him half as much as Birdie.

He brushed my fur with hands that trembled and made me want to shake them off like raindrops. But I didn't. My energy was just beginning to flag when we came to a wispy-haired lady in a wheelchair. Her hands were gnarled, but her eyes snapped and sparkled.

"Put him down right here," she said, pointing to her lap.

Mindy mostly preferred to set me up on a table that was level with their arms so they could pat me and brush me and have a proper visit. But the old lady said, "Please?" in the sweetest way, so Mindy gave in.

She set me gently in the lady's lap. The lady started to stroke my fur. Her hands were hard and bony. While she petted me, she talked to Mindy. Mindy listened, keeping one eye on me.

"He's such a cute little fellow," said the lady. "I just want to love him all up." She pulled me closer to her and started to hug me until my eyes bugged out. "Good, good, *good* doggie!" she said, squeezing me so hard that I let out a yelp.

Mindy's hand shot up. She signaled to the tall man. He ran over and gently pried the old girl's hands off of me. "Easy now, Mrs. Crawley. You don't want to hurt the little dog."

I tell you, I was shaking all over.

"It's okay, Rolf. Let's get you home," Mindy whispered in my ear. Then she said to the people still waiting to meet me, "I think Rolf's had enough for one day. He needs to go home and rest. We'll see you all soon."

When we got outside into the parking lot, Mindy stopped and stroked my back for a few moments. "Oh, Rolf! I should never have let you sit in her lap."

The door of the building opened up, and the tall man burst out and ran over to us.

"That was my fault," he said breathlessly. "I should have warned you about Mrs. Crawley. She may look weak, but she's got a grip like a bricklayer. She doesn't know her own strength anymore. When she grabs me sometimes, *I* want to bite her! But Rolf stayed cool and calm. That's a good, steady dog you've got there."

"Rolf's a *great* dog," Mindy said.

DUMB BOOK!

Mindy and I were in a new parking lot, having our Together Time. Inside the nearby building, I could hear children laughing and singing.

"We're just pinch-hitting today, Rolf," Mindy said. "Gail has a sick therapy dog we're subbing for. If you like it, we might add the school to our weekly rounds. But only if you like it. How does that sound?"

Mindy seemed happy and excited about our outing, so I was game.

Inside, we went into a glass-walled office, where Mindy announced us. The ladies there made a fuss over me. In a short time, a young man came to greet us.

"I'm Gavin. I'm in charge of special education here at Sweetbriar Primary School," he said as he shook Mindy's hand. "I'm so glad you and Rolf could make it. So far, the program's been very successful. The kids love working with the Reading Dog. And Rolf even looks like one of their favorite storybook characters. A certain big, red dog."

"Did you hear that, Rolf?" Mindy said to me. "You're going to be a Reading Dog today."

Lead on, my eyes told her. I trotted down the long polished hallway, following Mindy and Gavin.

Through the doors on either side, I spied small children sitting at desks. Everything, including the children, was low and close to the ground—just like me. I can't quite explain it, but I had a good feeling about the place.

"We're set up to work in the library," Gavin said, coming to a stop in front of a glass door. "There are no classes in here this period, so it'll be nice and quiet. Gail explained to you how it works?"

"I have Rolf lie down and stay in the dog bed. Then I hover just out of sight so I can listen to what's happening. I'm supposed to let the child and the dog work it out."

"The child and the dog and *the book*," Gavin said with a smile.

"Got it," said Mindy.

He pushed open the glass door. The room was

big and sunny and crowded with long, low shelves filled with the kinds of books Mindy kept in her study. There were small tables and chairs and stuffed animals and pictures hanging on the walls. The whole place had a comfortable, cheery feel. It was almost like home.

A lady sitting behind a big desk got up and bustled over to us.

"Hi! I'm Liz, the new librarian. Mindy, it's a pleasure to meet you. We have all your books in our collection. We'd love it if you could come in to do a signing sometime. Maybe talk about your work and draw some pictures?"

Mindy blushed. "Thanks for the invite! I'd be happy to," she said.

We followed Gavin to a spot between two bookshelves, where there were some floor cushions next to a dog bed.

"This is the Cozy Book Nook," said Gavin. "We here at Sweetbriar like to think of it as a safe place for learning."

Mindy led me over to the dog bed. My nose twitched and picked up the scents of the dogs who had sat here before me. She asked me to Sit, then Lie Down. Then Stay. So far, this was easy peasy.

Then Mindy walked away. But she didn't go far.

Gavin returned with a child who dragged his feet. Under his arm, he carried a big book.

"Ryan, this is Rolf. Rolf wants to hear a story this morning, don't you, Rolf?"

I looked up at the boy. He seemed nervous. So I wagged my tail to break the ice.

"Hold out your hand to him, Ryan," said Gavin. "So he can say hello."

The boy stuck out his hand. I buried my nose

in his palm. It smelled like bacon and eggs.

"*Eeew!*" said the boy, wiping his hand on his pants. "He licked me!"

"He's friendly," said Gavin. "That's because he's happy to be here with you."

"Yeah?" said Ryan. "Is it true he's only got three legs? Can he stand up so I can see his stump?"

"I think he'd rather lie there and listen to you read to him," said Gavin.

"How come they didn't get him one of those nifty bionic legs?" Ryan asked. "Or else an awesome peg leg, like the pirate in the book I brought? *Arrrrrrrghhh,*" he said to me.

I cocked my head and growled playfully at him.

Gavin laughed. "I think he just said *aaargh* back to you, Ryan. That's 'cause you two are mateys."

Ryan sank down into the cushions. I settled deeper into the dog bed, keeping an eye on him.

"Is he really gonna listen to me?" Ryan asked.

"To every word," said Gavin.

"If you say so," said the boy. He sounded doubtful.

Ryan watched Gavin leave. Then he opened the book. "I'm warning you," he said to me, "I can't read for beans."

I didn't know what he meant and I didn't care. I gave him my most eager look. I thumped my tail against the bed.

"Don't look so excited."

I stopped thumping and put my head down on my paws. If that was the way he wanted to play it, I would take it down a notch.

"Okay, here goes nothing," said the boy.

He stuttered and stammered and flinched as if something hurt. He turned the pages very slowly. I watched and waited and listened. Honestly, I would have loved to close my eyes and nap, but I knew my job was to stay awake.

At last, the boy slammed the book shut. He was panting, as if he had run a race. "Phew!" he said. "I did it! That was a first."

I crawled over and licked his face, which tasted salty with sweat and traces of bacon.

"Thanks for listening, Rolf," he said. "Maybe I can read you another book sometime."

Ryan patted me until Gavin came back and walked him out. Mindy beamed at me and told me I had done well.

A week later, we returned to the Cozy Book Nook because the regular dog was still sick. I settled into the bed. For the longest time, no one came. I was just dozing off when I heard the loud tramping of feet.

I leapt up.

A little girl with a tangle of pale, wispy hair was standing there glaring at me. There was a deep, angry crease between her eyes and a book clutched in her fists.

Oh-oh, Rolf, I said to myself. *You may have met your match.*

"Katy Rose!" said Gavin. "This is Rolf. You need to be *nice* to him. He is a very kind and special dog. He's here to read with you. If you give it a chance, you might even have fun."

Katy Rose curled her lip and growled. "Fun? Reading? You've got to be *kidding* me. Reading's no fun at all. Reading's *work*."

Gavin sighed wearily. "Well, try, at least, Katy Rose. For Rolf's sake."

I sat down on the bed and kept a wary eye on Katy Rose.

She plopped herself down on the cushions. Then she yanked open the book and stared down at it with eyes blazing.

She began: " 'Dog. B-i-g dog. L-i-t-t . . . ' "

Her face got red. Her fingertips pinched the pages. Her hands trembled. "Dumb book!" she cried out. "Who wants to read a story about a bunch of dumb dogs running around, anyway?"

She lifted the book over her head and hurled it
across the floor.

I stared at the book lying there. So she wanted
to play fetch? I was up for it. I rose from the bed
and walked over to the book. I picked it up in my
teeth and took it back to her.

"Didn't you hear me?" she said between clenched teeth. *"I said it's a dumb book and I don't want to read it!"*

She snatched it from my jaws and flung it away from her again.

I walked over to fetch the book and return it. This was going to be fun. I could play fetch all morning.

I guess she could, too, because she kept on throwing that book. Katy Rose had a good, strong arm. The book was starting to look a little ragged. I'm glad I wasn't a book. This Katy Rose was hard on books.

"Don't you get it, dog?" she said when I had brought the book back to her yet another time. "I can't read, and I'm never going to learn. *I'm dumb!*"

She flung the book again. It hit the wall and split into two pieces.

I went and picked up one piece, then the other. When I returned them to Katy Rose, her face was buried in her hands and her shoulders shook. I laid the pieces on the floor in front of her and wriggled onto her lap. She threw her arms around me and wept. It wasn't long before the top of my head was soaked with tears.

When Gavin returned and Mindy came to get me, Katy Rose dried her face on my ear. She asked in a small voice, "Can I come back and try again? I didn't get to finish the story. Rolf wants to hear it. Don't you, Rolf?"

I touched my nose to Katy Rose's salty cheek.

"Rolf kissed you!" said Gavin. "He must like you a lot."

"I don't know why," said Katy Rose. "Nobody likes me. I'm dumb."

I kissed her again.

"Well, Rolf obviously disagrees," said Mindy. "And I'll have you know that Rolf is an excellent judge of character."

We went back to the Nook the following day. Can you guess who my first reader was? That's right: Katy Rose. I braced myself for another endless round of fetch. But maybe her arm was tired.

"Okay," she said to me when we were alone. "No more throwing books. I'm going to read it to you . . . if it takes me all day."

Instead of lying in my bed, I sat with her on the cushions, my chin propped on her knee. I stared at her with adoring eyes. It wasn't hard. There was something about this unhappy child that I liked. She made me want to root for her.

"Okay, Rolf. Here I go."

Someone had taped the book back together.

She opened it and held it so that I could see the pictures. Not that I cared to see them. I cared about Katy Rose. Her shoulders were stiff, and her hands shook. Was she going to turn on the waterworks again?

It was slow and painful going at first. Katy Rose stopped for long moments and struggled to get the words out. Sometimes the words wouldn't come. Then her fists would bunch and her teeth would grind, and she would hold her breath.

When she did that, I would inch my way further into her lap and pant close to her face, reminding her to breathe. She would pet me and say, "Okay, Rolf, I get it." Then she would take a deep breath and give it another try.

A while later, I looked up to see Gavin and Mindy standing there with big smiles on their faces. By that time, I had climbed all the way onto Katy Rose's lap. My head was tucked beneath her chin.

"The end," she said as she closed the book.

KATY ROSE'S PLAN

We stopped visiting the school. That was okay by me. Mindy and I were plenty busy and I knew it was just a temporary job. But I did wonder what had happened to Katy Rose.

Then one day, Mindy and I were walking downtown when I saw her!

"Isn't that Katy Rose?" Mindy said, pointing up ahead. "Should we go say hi to her?"

I wagged my tail yes, and we walked over to

her. I noticed that the snarls in her hair had been untangled. Finally, someone had groomed this child! And the deep, angry crease between her eyes? It was all smoothed out. Katy Rose was different. I think she was happier. A big, strong man was holding her hand.

"Dad," she said to him, "remember the dog I told you about? The amazingly sweet and smart Reading Dog?"

"The one who was such a good listener?" he asked, and burst into a smile.

"Mindy and Rolf," said Katy Rose, "meet my dad."

Katy's dad was a tall, bashful man with eyes that were kind and just the slightest bit sad. The muscles on his arms bulged, and his hands were large and rough. I made this discovery when he leaned down to pet me—very gently.

"Glad I could finally meet Rolf the Wonder Dog."

"*And* Mindy, the Wonder . . . *Lady,*" Katy Rose added with a grin.

He said to Mindy, "I'm Donald Bartlett. Katy Rose's teacher says she's made a real breakthrough in her reading. And last Friday, she got a star for reading more books during the week than any other student."

"Happy to hear it," Mindy said.

Was it me, or was Mindy the Wonder Lady blushing?

He said, "The fact is, I haven't seen her this happy since, well . . ."

"Since my mom died," Katy Rose put in, "sixteen months, two weeks, and three days ago."

"I didn't realize . . . ," Mindy said, sounding flustered.

"That's okay," said Katy Rose. "We're doing pretty good, except when Dad tries to cook. Then the house gets kind of smoky."

"It's true, I'm afraid," said Donald. "But I'm very good at takeout."

Everyone laughed.

A while later, we met Katy Rose and her father at Paws to Refresh. Mindy said, "There are pretty strict rules about therapy dogs and their partners socializing with their clients. But since Rolf is no longer your therapy dog, I think it's okay for us to be friends."

Katy Rose and I spent most of the time under the table. Meanwhile, above the table, Mindy and Donald were getting along like gangbusters. The more they talked and laughed, the bigger Katy Rose's smile grew.

"I've got a plan," she whispered to me.

We began to visit the Bartletts' house often. Soon, Mindy was even cooking them meals. They would all sit down to eat at the big table while I lay happily at their feet.

Mindy and I continued to make our rounds at the hospital's rehab floor and at the skilled nursing facility.

Sometimes, Katy Rose came to see us at our house. She visited Mindy's studio and always said very nice things about the drawings tacked to her board.

"I've read all your books," she told Mindy. "I like the one about the bomb-sniffing dog the best. Are you going to write one about a therapy dog like Rolf?"

"I might," said Mindy. She winked at me.

Katy Rose even helped to keep me spiffy.

"I brush him daily," Mindy explained. "It's important that I stay on top of his grooming, including his ears and eyes. I keep his nails trimmed, too. I wouldn't want him to accidentally scratch anyone."

"It's a lot of work, taking care of a therapy dog," Katy Rose said.

"It is, but I think of it as time spent with my bestest bud," she said, giving me a gentle squeeze.

"You really love Rolf, don't you?" said Katy Rose. "And you guys lead a busy life. Do you think there could ever be room in your life for anyone else?"

Mindy smiled at Katy Rose and smoothed her hair. "If the right person—or people—were to come along, I'd be more than happy to make room. So would Rolf. Wouldn't you, Rolf?"

That was my cue to wag.

There came a time when Mindy had to travel east on what she called business. I knew she couldn't take me with her, so I worried about who would take care of me while she was gone. But I didn't have to worry for long.

"I'll be back before you know it, Rolf," Mindy said. "Gail has found someone to sub for us this week. And Katy Rose and Don will take good care of you while I'm gone."

Confident that Mindy would soon return, I happily stayed behind with my friends.

Katy Rose and I knew how to keep busy. She would pile pillows and blankets in the center of the living room floor for us to burrow in. As she explained, "My dad builds houses; I build forts."

During my visit, I shared her bed, too. I had always slept on the floor beside the bed of my human companions. But Katy Rose insisted I join her, not only *up on* the bed but *underneath* the covers. She was a very thoughtful girl. She even rigged a ramp out of cushions so that I wouldn't be tempted to leap up or down and hurt my back.

At night, after Don had tucked us in, we would burrow down deep together. She would switch on a flashlight and read to me in a whisper until both of us dropped off to sleep.

When Mindy returned from her business, there was a great deal of hugging and kissing. I went home with her, and life resumed its comfy routine. Days in the studio, walks to the Dog Park and the café, visits to rehab and skilled nursing. With increasing frequency, Mindy and I would drop over at Katy Rose's house to visit.

One day, Katy Rose and I were burrowed deep in the fort, when we heard Mindy say, "Yoo-hoo! Anybody home?"

Katy Rose and I poked our heads out. Don and Mindy were standing there, both looking a little sheepish.

Katy Rose put a pretend frown on her face. "We were very busy. This had better be important."

"We think it is," said Don. Then, looking a little lost, he turned to Mindy. "Honey, do you want to start?"

"All right," said Mindy, clasping her hands nervously in front of her. "Katy Rose, you know that over the last few months I've gotten to know you and your father very well."

Katy Rose nodded. Her arm went around me. "And we've gotten to know you guys, too. And we like you a whole lot. Right, Dad?"

"Right," said Don slowly. "I'd say more than *like*. The fact is, Katy Rose, I've fallen in love with Mindy. And, lucky guy that I am, turns out she loves me back."

Mindy put in quickly, "I know no one can ever replace your mother. And I wouldn't expect to. But

I'd like to try, if you'll give me a chance, to be a wife to your dad, and the very best kind of stepmother to you."

"What about Rolf?" Katy Rose wanted to know.

"I think Rolf will be very happy." Mindy smiled at me. "After all, it gives him more people to love."

Katy Rose's eyes grew bright. "Can he sleep with me every night?"

Mindy hesitated. "Of course he can. If it's all right with your father . . . and Rolf."

"When's the wedding?" Katy Rose asked.

"We haven't gotten quite that far yet," Don said. "We were waiting for your approval."

"You have my approval. And Rolf's, too. So let's start planning! I get to be the flower girl, right?" she asked.

"We wouldn't have it any other way," Mindy said, laughing.

"And Rolf gets to be ring bearer?" Katy Rose said.

Mindy smiled. "I think Rolf will make a very spiffy ring bearer."

Katy Rose leapt to her feet and pumped her fist in the air. *"Yes! Yes! Yes!"* She began to dance around our Reading Fort. "My plan worked! It really worked! I'm the luckiest girl in the world. I got a new mom *and* a new dog all at once!"

Hot diggity dog! I did a three-legged jig to a lively round of *Rolf! Rolf! Rolf!*

That is how my pack grew to include two more people who were just as wonderful as my Mindy. Mindy and Don went on to have two children

together, and the pack kept growing.

Mindy was too busy being a mom, and so our therapy visits had to come to an end. But my paws were quite full with the young ones, as you can imagine.

I'll have to cut this entry short. I hear Katy Rose calling my name. After putting it off and making all sorts of excuses, that girl is finally sitting down to fill out those college applications of hers. Just like I once helped her learn to read, she'll need my encouragement to stick with it and get the job done. I'll be there to support and encourage her. Haven't I always been?

I have to say, after all these years, it's great to still be needed.

Once a therapy dog, always a therapy dog.

APPENDIX

What Is a Therapy Dog?

As early as the ninth century in Gheel, Belgium, animals were used in the therapy of people with disabilities. In the 1700s, the York Retreat in England found that when patients with mental illness learned to care for animals, physical restraints and harsh drugs could be avoided.

A major advance came about in the 1950s at Yeshiva University, in New York City, when Dr. Boris Levinson discovered that if he brought his Shetland sheepdog, Jingles, to therapy sessions, he could make significant progress working with emotionally disturbed children.

In the 1970s, two national therapy dog

organizations, Delta Society's Pet Partners Program and Therapy Dogs International (TDI), started in the United States. In the 1980s and '90s, several other national therapy dog organizations were formed, including Love on a Leash, Bright and Beautiful Therapy Dogs, and St. John Ambulance in Canada. Beginning in the 2000s, there was a dramatic shift when many therapy dogs began being registered with local nonprofit organizations.

No matter what the organization, therapy dogs visit thousands of hospitals, schools, libraries, assisted-living facilities, nursing homes, hospices, disaster areas, and funeral homes offering love and comfort. There are even dogs that visit college campuses during exam weeks to lower the stress level of students.

No one can really say how these animals work their magic, but the good they do has been borne

A therapy dog at work

out by scientific studies. Contact with a dog releases chemicals in a person's brain that decrease blood pressure, relieve stress, and boost spirits. In other words, dogs are good medicine!

In order to become registered with a therapy dog organization, many groups require that the dog pass the American Kennel Club's Canine Good Citizen™ (CGC) test. Before the test, a dog's owner will be asked to sign a pledge that states that he or she agrees to take care of the dog's health and safety, exercise and training, and overall quality of life. The handler also vows to clean up after the dog in public and to never let the dog interfere with the rights of others.

The test consists of the following:

- Accepting a friendly stranger without shyness or resentment
- Sitting politely for petting from a friendly stranger
- Holding still for grooming by handler or others
- Walking attentively on a loose lead, halting, and turning left and right
- Passing through a crowd without showing either shyness toward strangers or an excessive amount of enthusiasm
- Responding to training: sitting, lying down, staying until released
- Coming when called

- Behaving politely around other dogs
- Not overreacting to distractions, loud noises, and unusual sights, such as wheelchairs or crutches
- Being left with a trusted stranger

The next step is to pass a therapy organization's therapy-specific test—including the performance of tasks such as "go say hello" to a patient and "paws up" (standing with paws up on a stool so a patient in bed can reach the dog)—and to register with a group that places volunteer teams in therapy settings. Reputable groups carry insurance, which is important in case anything should happen to either the dogs or the people in the course of these volunteer visits.

Therapy dogs are sometimes mistaken for service dogs, but they are not the same thing. Service dogs have been specially trained to assist disabled persons in a one-on-one capacity. Under the Americans with Disabilities Act, service dogs are legally permitted to go anywhere their people need to go. No such laws apply to therapy dogs. While they are not always required to, therapy dogs often wear their organization's official vests. When vests are worn, they are designed to fit the dog comfortably and still allow for lots of cuddling and hugs. After all, therapy dogs are about hugs—and the healing power of unconditional dog love.

For an extensive list of national and local therapy organizations that you and your dog can join, visit this site:

• akc.org/dog-owners/training/akc-therapy-dog-program

Find information about the American Kennel Club's Canine Good Citizen™ program here:

• akc.org/dog-owners/training/canine-good-citizen

About the Dachshund

Built long and low to the ground, with short legs, broad chest, drop ears, and sharp snout, the dachshund might, at first glance, seem a comical character. But make no mistake about it: this is a well-balanced, muscular, alert, and highly intelligent breed.

Isn't he handsome?

Known as an earthdog, it has been bred and trained over centuries to dig and find animals that live under the earth, like rabbits, groundhogs, voles, and badgers. German engravings dating back as far as five hundred years show such dogs tearing up the countryside hunting for badgers, the bane of farmers. Digging deep into the underground dens, or setts, of the ferocious badger required strength, persistence, and bravery—traits this dog has in spades. Originally brought to the United States in 1870 to hunt rabbits, the dachshund was first registered with the American Kennel Club in 1885. Year after year, it is among the most popular breeds.

Dachshunds come in two sizes: standard, at sixteen to thirty-two pounds, and miniature, at eleven pounds and under. Dachshunds have three coat types—smooth, wirehaired, and long-haired—

and come in a variety of colors and markings. Unfortunately, because of the length of their spines, they are prone to back problems and vulnerable to injury. But handled properly, they can live happy, active lives.

Many people enter their dachsies in shows for conformation (form), obedience, agility, and field and earthdog trials.

John Wayne, Joan Crawford, Clark Gable, Clint Eastwood, E. B. White, George Harrison, Napoléon Bonaparte, and Albert Einstein have all been proud owners of dachshunds. Her Majesty, Queen Elizabeth II of England has bred her prize corgis with dachsies to create an adorable new breed called dorgis.

Get more information about the dachshund:

•akc.org/dog-breeds/dachshund

Owning a Dachshund

E. B. White once said, "Being the owner of dachshunds, to me a book on dog discipline becomes a volume of inspired humor. Every sentence is a riot." What he means is that the average dachshund, because of the sheer strength of its will, is a bit of a challenge to train. But with persistence and patience, a dachshund can learn to be obedient—which is to say, to follow you instead of its nose.

The dachshund is a special dog and requires special considerations. Highly sensitive to scents and sounds, it can take very little to set a dachsie off and running. And, as you've heard from Rolf, the dachshund has a rather *big* bark. Given the breed's innate curiosity and love of digging, this is not a dog that you will want to leave unsupervised

And they're off!

for very long in your backyard. It will enthusiastically dig up your flower beds and think it's doing you a favor. The dog might be strong and vigorous but does have a weakness. Because of the way the dachshund is made, it is prone to back problems. It is important to learn to hold the dog horizontally so that its spine gets proper support, with one hand beneath the hind legs and another under the chest.

H. L. Mencken famously said, "A dachshund is a half-dog high and a dog-and-a-half long." But as Mindy, Katy Rose, and thousands of other happy human companions will attest, a dachshund is *all* heart.

For more information about living with a dachshund, go to this site:

• dachshundclubofamerica.org

Tripods and Two-Leggers

A tripod—or "tripawd"—is a dog with three legs. The loss of the leg can be due to cancer, birth defect, or, as was the case with Rolf, an accident.

Many dogs do fine with just three legs.

And, just like Rolf, most dogs get around remarkably well on three legs. With the right care and support from you, a tripod can thrive. As with all dogs, it's important that tripods not be allowed to put on extra weight, which can overtax the joints and bring on arthritis. Keeping paw pads healthy and clean and nails short is also key, since tripods are prone to slip and slide. Minimizing the number of slippery surfaces in your home is a good idea. And applying special wax or cream to the dog's paw pads can help him maintain traction. These caring measures aside, it might be tempting to further pamper a three-legged dog. But it's important to trust in your dog's ability to cope and thrive. Just let your dog be a dog.

There are some tripods, however, who, for health reasons, can't manage on their own. For these dogs, there are wheeled supports, which are available through animal hospitals, veterinarians, and animal rehabilitation centers. And dogs that have lost two legs are dependent for their mobility on such devices. These carts, especially if they are custom-fit, are expensive items to buy, but they do improve the dog's quality of life.

This dog is ready to rock and roll!

For more information on tripods and wheeled supports, go to these sites:

- amcny.org/blog/2013/03/05/tripawds -awareness-day
- acvs.org/small-animal/limb-amputation
- tripawds.com/2008/11/17/the-top-10-questions -about-amputation-for-dogs